This L...rn / rene...v date s... ...ongs to:

_____

_____

_____

To Mandy — JT

LITTLE TIGER PRESS
1 The Coda Centre, 189 Munster Road, London SW6 6AW
www.littletigerpress.com

First published in 2013
This edition published 2013

Text and illustrations copyright © Jack Tickle 2013

Jack Tickle has asserted his right to
be identified as the author and illustrator of this work
under the Copyright, Designs and Patents Act, 1988

A CIP catalogue record for this book is available
from the British Library

ISBN 978-1-84895-546-2 • LTP/1800/0493/0912
2 4 6 8 10 9 7 5 3 1

Look Out, Ladybird!

Jack Tickle

LITTLE TIGER PRESS
London

Ladybird was
learning to fly.
But she wasn't very
good at it yet.

So she practised all day.

And she practised all night.

Ooops!

Eeek!

Aagh!

"Whoopsie-doops!
I'll try again tomorrow,"
she said to herself.

The next day Ladybird
climbed up a rock and
took a great big leap.

Wheeeeeee

But. . .

...Ladybird tumble-bumbled onto Elephant's

head.

TOOOOOOOOT!

"Look out, Ladybird!"
he trumpeted.
"Oops!" she gasped.
"Sorry about that."

Ladybird slid down

Elephant's trunk.

"Can't stop – I'm learning to fly," she cried, zig-zagging down to the grass.

Tiger's tail!

RAAAARGH!

"Look out, Ladybird!"
he roared.

"Oooooh! Fuzzy-wuzzy
tummy!" she giggled.

"Stop tickling!" Tiger chuckled, flicking his tail.

Eeeeek!

Ladybird cried, as
she looped-the-loop
towards the water.

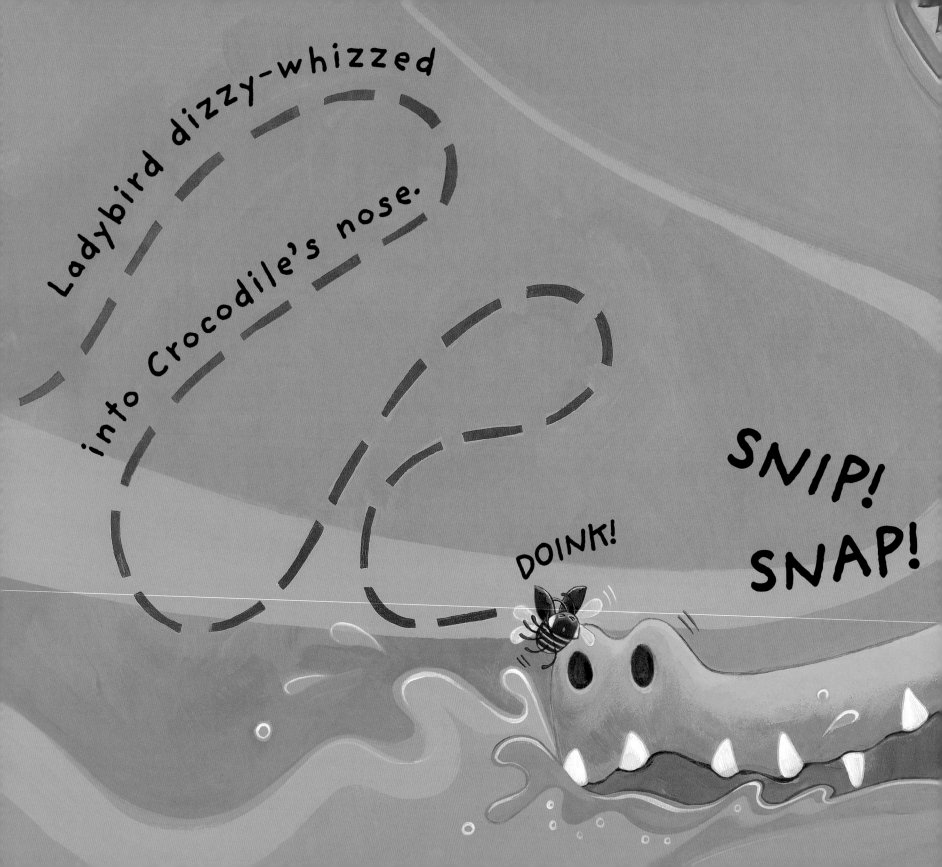

"Look out, Ladybird!"
he smiled.
But she wobbled off
wildly towards the
trees.

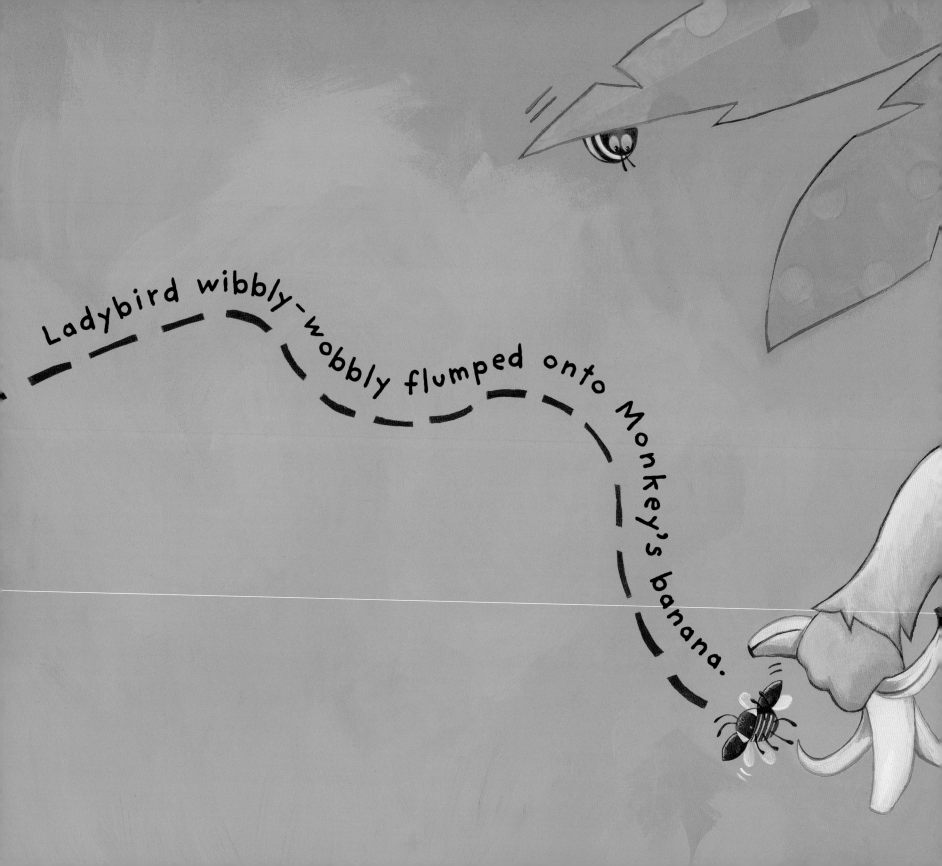

Ladybird wibbly-wobbly flumped onto Monkey's banana.

OOO-OOO!

"Look out, Ladybird!"
she chattered.

"Oh this is terrible!"
Ladybird sniffed.

"I've bumped into Elephant..."

"I'll *never* learn how to fly!"
sniffed Ladybird.
"Go on, give it another try!"
Monkey grinned.
"Another try?" thought
Ladybird.

So she flapped her
tiny wings with all her might.
And she didn't . . .

tumble-bumble

or dizzy-whizz

or wibble-wobble.

She zoomed **STRAIGHT** up, up, up into the sky. Until . . .

"Look at me FLY!"

THE END

Look out . . . for more exciting Little Tiger books!

I Don't Want to go to Bed!
Julie Sykes
Tim Warnes

Can You See SASSOON?
Sam Usher

Duck Says DON'T!
Alison Ritchie · Hannah George

The Very Lazy Ladybird
Isobel Finn & Jack Tickle

Bright Stanley Double Trouble
Matt Buckingham

Super-Duper Dudley!
Sue Mongredien

For information regarding any of the above titles or for our catalogue, please contact us:
Little Tiger Press, 1 The Coda Centre, 189 Munster Road, London SW6 6AW
Tel: 020 7385 6333 • Fax: 020 7385 7333
E-mail: info@littletiger.co.uk • www.littletigerpress.com